THE ADVENTURES
OF PEANUT POWER

Peanut Power Races to Nome

Written By Dennis M. Vecera

Illustrated by Cris Rodriguez

PUBLICATION CONSULTANTS

We Believe In The Power Of Authors

PO Box 221974 Anchorage, Alaska 99522-1974

books@publicationconsultants.com—www.publicationconsultants.com

ISBN 978-1-59433-963-9
Library of Congress Control Number: 2020910842

Copyright 2020 Dennis M. Vecera
First Edition

Illustrations by Cris Rodriguez of Creative Illustrations Studio

THERE'S A NEW SUPERHERO IN TOWN...AND HIS NAME IS PEANUT POWER.

Published in Cooperation With Publication Consultants
8370 Eleusis Drive
Anchorage, Alaska 99502
https://publicationconsultants.com
Email: books@publicationconsultants.com

Salty Nut Publishing Co.
3000 Dawson St.
Anchorage, AK 99503
Tel. (907) 575-1125
e-mail: dvecera@gci.net
www.saltynutpublishingcompany.com

The Adventures of Peanut Power: Peanut Power Races to Nome is dedicated to the memory of my dad and to my amazing mom, both of whom have always been there to support me. My greatest superheroes!

THE HISTORY OF THE IDITAROD SLED DOG RACE

The Iditarod Trail was first used when the Alaskan gold rush began in the 1880s. Towns came alive as gold was discovered. One such town was called Iditarod, named for the Indian word haidi-tarod, which means "a distant place." The Iditarod Trail became a way to reach these distant places. It was full of swamps in the summer, but in the winter it was a major transportation route for the dog sled teams that most people used to transport mail and goods. It continued to be used until the mid 1920s.

The use of reliable airplanes in the late 1920s signaled the beginning of the end for the dog team as the standard mode of transportation for carrying the mail and other goods. In the 1960s dog teams were replaced by the "iron dog." The use of the snowmobile was the final blow to the use of the dog team, which resulted in mass abandonment of dog teams across the state. Mushing stories once told were forgotten too.

In 1964, a committee in Wasilla was formed to look into the historical events in Alaska over the past century. The committee was in charge of coming up with an event to celebrate the 100th anniversary of the purchase of Alaska from Russia. Dorothy Page, who chaired the committee, conceived the idea of a sled dog race over the historically significant Iditarod Trail. Joe Redington Sr. was her first real support. He felt this centennial race would help in their quest to preserve the historic gold rush and mail route between Seward and Iditarod. Redington also wanted to preserve the Alaskan husky and the sled dog culture in Alaska.

The Iditarod Trail Sled Dog Race is a reconstruction of the freight route to Nome and commemorates the part that sled dogs played in the settlement of Alaska. The Iditarod Trail Sled Dog Race was not started to honor the Serum Run of 1925, nor is it run each year as a commemoration of the Serum Run as often falsely reported.

In 1973, the first official Iditarod Sled Dog Race ran from Anchorage to Nome. The race was called "The Last Great Race on Earth," and Joe Redington Sr. and Dorothy Page became known as the "Father and Mother of the Iditarod." Today, the race continues, and for Peanut Power and his team the adventure begins. Join Peanut Power and his team as they race along each checkpoint to Nome, to raise money for the sick children of Alaska.

It was 32 degrees in Peanutville, a small community just 48 miles south of Anchorage. Looking at the thermometer, Peanut Power knew the temperature was perfect for a sled dog race. Peanut Power smiled as he thought about the ceremonial start in Anchorage and racing over 900 miles from Willow to Nome in the Iditarod Trail Sled Dog Race.

His 13 dogs were excited too. The team trained hard all summer. With microchips transplanted, they were ready for the longest, hardest and most respected race in the world. They were ready to race across frozen tundra, through fierce snow storms and wrestle with temperatures cold enough to freeze kibble solid. The dogs were excited to be part of "The Last Great Race on Earth."

In the 1920s Peanut Power's grandpa, Saltynut, used his team of Alaskan huskies to help miners transport their gold from mine to town. To this day, Salty's team is remembered as the fastest and most powerful team in the world. Peanut Power's dogs were a new breed of husky. They did not like dog food, only peanut butter. Peanut butter cookies and peanut butter biscuits made the dogs happy and satisfied.

Peanut Power found his dogs when they were orphan puppies. One rainy spring day he saw all 13 of them huddled inside an abandoned peanut shell on the outskirts of Peanutville. It was said that the pups' parents were trampled by a powerful, mean moose. Only Walnut, the oldest of the pups, had actually seen the moose because he was the only one whose eyes had opened. Peanut Power loved these dogs even if they were the nuttiest looking pups he had ever seen.

Naming the puppies was easy as peanut butter pie. He named them Almond, Brazil, Cashew, Chestnut, Filbert (Hazelnut's fraternal twin), Hazelnut, Hickory, Macadamia, Pecan, Piñon, Pistachio, Walnut and the runt of the litter, Goober. He was covered with mud when Peanut Power found him. Goober reminded him of the chocolate covered candy you buy at the movies. Peanut Power had a special string of dogs. They were dedicated, committed, strong and didn't mind working hard. They were true litter mates who worked together as a team.

Peanut Power knew before he could enter the Iditarod he had to teach his dogs the commands the other mushers used. When he said "Gee" which means "turn right," his dogs would bark. When he said "Haw" which means "turn left" his dogs would stop and sit. So Peanut Power used "creamy" for right turns and "crunchy" for "left." The usual command to start is "Hike!" or "Let's go!" But for Peanut Power's special litter, the command was "peanut butter." And, believe it or not, when Peanut Power yelled "whoa!" the dogs stopped, looked, and listened.

In March of the following year, Peanut Power loaded his dogs into the dog boxes on his peanut shaped truck for the hour-long drive to Anchorage. Peanut Power made sure he had plenty of peanut butter, plus snowshoes, ax, shell sleeping bag, a cooker, three gallon pot, fuel, harness and cable gangline. In addition, he needed eight booties for each dog, an insulated dog coat for each dog, veterinarian notebook in which each dog's condition is recorded at checkpoints, and peanut sunscreen for the sunny days when light would glare off the snow. It was two days before the race. Peanut

Power and the other 49 mushers drew numbers from a mukluk to see who would break trail or follow last in the pack. Peanut Power drew seventh position. He was proud his grandpa was given the honorary "Number 1." The people of Alaska still remember one of the world's best dog mushers. Peanut Power's grandpa was commemorated not only for helping the miners, but for racing against time to get the much needed serum to the sick people of Nome. In 1925 he saved many lives before the epidemic took his own life.

Peanut Power took Goober, the runt of the litter, for the ride. He said, "I will keep you with the rest of the family. We will run this race together." Peanut Power also took his beautiful French-roasted wife, Honeynut, as his IditaRider. Honeynut won the bid to be a rider in a musher's sled from the start line on Fourth Avenue at D Street all the way to the Campbell Air Strip just 11 miles away. Goober was unhappy. "Peanut Power," Goober whined, "I do not want to ride on the sled. I want to help my brothers and sisters."

"You are too small and weak to run. In a couple more years you will be big enough to lead this team to the finish line," exclaimed Peanut Power, giving Goober a paw shake and a reassuring nod.

On the first Saturday in March, thousands of spectators lined the streets of downtown Anchorage to meet, cheer and photograph the mushers, and to see the start of the "Greatest race on earth." Peanut Power was cheered on by his friends: Watermelon Man, Propeller Man, Buckey Beaver, Peanut Puff and Dr. Bandage, who would help tend to the needs of the dogs. His son, Supernut Power, also came to encourage his dad and favorite superhero.

Two minutes after musher six left the starting line, Peanut Power's team sped off and headed towards the Campbell Airstrip.

After the short ceremonial run, Peanut Power loaded his dogs into his truck. The next day they drove a little over 70 miles to Willow.

The following day, Sunday, the mushers lined up for the restart of the race. Peanut Power and his team were ready to start the race from Willow to Nome. Goober was

getting antsy again. He wanted to run with the pack. "Peanut Power, when am I going to help pull the sled?" pleaded Goober.

"Someday you will make a fine race dog, but for now ride with me. Help me cheer on your brothers and sisters," said Peanut Power.

Before the start of the race, Peanut Power talked with his dogs, one by one. "I believe in every one of you. Do your best! Walnut, you are the lead dog. Get us to Nome!" Walnut and the rest of the pack yelped with excitement. "Peanut Power, I want to help! But what can I do?" asked Watermelon Man.

"There is one thing you can do," said Peanut Power.

"What is it?" questioned Watermelon Man.

"The salt on my sled has caused the ice to melt on my runners. Could I get you to spray some cold water on them? The cold will make the water freeze. Ice on the runners will make the sled go faster," replied Peanut Power. So with Watermelon Man's special ability, he sprayed water on the runners of Peanut Power's sled.

Propeller Man helped by flying along the trail and making sure no one ended up missing or was attacked by a moose. "I sure hope the strong winds don't blow and cover up the trails with snow," sighed Propeller Man.

"Don't worry, Propeller Man," declared Supernut Power. "I am going to ride my iron peanut. Buckey Beaver and I will break trail. We will clear branches off the path and pack the snow as we go. The good news is the trail is visibly marked with 8-foot high posts with reflectors every few hundred yards to mark its path. Peanut Power has a GPS receiver too so he can keep track of the mushers' positions."The beautiful Honeynut was worried. "Oh darling, please take care of yourself," she cried with tears in her big brown eyes. "I love you and wish you the best of luck." "I love you too! Meet me at McGrath for dinner!" announced Peanut Power, giving her a big hug.

At 2:00 p.m. the first musher departed on his way to Nome. In two minute intervals, the mushers left one by one. After the musher wearing bib number 6 charged out of the gate, Peanut Power brought his dogs to the starting point with the help of his friends. Peanut Power approached each dog. "Are we ready? Today is the day we have been waiting for. Let's do it!" whispered Peanut Power into their furry ears. And with that, Walnut, Filbert, Cashew and the rest of the pack leapt and jumped, showing their eagerness to be off. The countdown began, "Ten, nine, eight, seven, six, five, four, three, two, one!" Peanut Power yelled, "Peanut Butter!" He was off. His dogs were pulling harder than ever before. They were doing what they were born to do—race.

23

It was time to check into Skwenta. Peanut Power was tired, and so were his dogs. Goober was curled into a ball and fast asleep. Peanut Power arrived at the checkpoint. The veterinarian, Dr. Quadruped, and Dr. Bandage checked each dog to make sure they were fit and healthy. "Peanut Power, your dogs are in excellent shape. How do you keep their coats so shiny and beautiful?" asked the veterinarian.

"My dogs like a special kind of food that has the right kinds of oil in it. It is high in protein," said Peanut Power. And with that, Peanut Power dished out two pounds of warm peanut butter to each dog. He then lay down a bale of straw for his dogs to sleep on. The dogs ate and then slept.

Peanut Power knew he had to use strategy to do well in the race. He called his good friend Watermelon Man. "Watermelon Man, come in. Do you read me?"

"Yes, Peanut Power what is it?" answered Watermelon Man.

"What is the best way to win this race?" inquired Peanut Power.

"If you want to win this race, you must keep a steady pace," Watermelon Man replied. "If the wind blows, you must learn to ride with the wind. You must know when to take breaks to eat or rest. Deciding how long to sleep or rest is also important. You must listen to and trust your dogs. Some dogs will need to ride in the sled. This lets them rest without stopping. Good instincts and common sense will help you win."

In the middle of the night, Goober pressed his cold little black nose against Peanut Power's cheek. "Peanut Power, is it time to get up? I am ready to be part of the team!" insisted Goober. Peanut Power quickly got up and dressed in layers to keep the Arctic winds off, and assembled his team. They were eager as ever to continue the race to Nome. However, Peanut Power was not convinced that Goober should run with the team.

Signing out with a race official, Peanut Power and his team headed down the trail. It was snowing hard, and soon the trail became hard to see as they passed through Finger Lake and headed towards Rainy Pass. The dogs barked and howled as they approached the infamous gorge. Goober hid under his blanket. Something out there was scaring the dogs. All of a sudden, and without warning, a huge moose plunged towards the team. Walnut cried, "It's him! It's him! It's the same moose that attacked my parents." The moose, Dalzell, was the biggest and meanest moose in Alaska.

Dalzell romped and stomped over the helpless team, and then disappeared as quickly as he had appeared. The lead dog, Walnut, was badly hurt. Filbert, Cashew and Almond had been trampled, also. They couldn't go on.

Peanut Power was just getting out his peanut radio to call for help when Propeller Man, Dr. Bandage and Supernut Power showed up and treated the wounded dogs. Dr. Bandage loaded the dogs into an Iditarod Air Force bush plane and had them flown to a dog clinic in Fairbanks. Propeller Man scouted for Dalzell before any other musher was injured. An hour later he reported back to Peanut Power. "I could not find Dalzell, but he couldn't have gone far. The snow is much too deep," said Propeller Man.

Peanut Power had to stop Dalzell before Dalzell attacked again. He knew it was important to place high enough in the race so he could win some prize money to help the sick children. However, it was also his duty to protect humankind.

Soon 30 mushers had passed Peanut Power. Peanut Power was relieved to see these 30 mushers pass safely. But how was he going to find Dalzell? Propeller Man reported seeing no sign of the huge moose. Peanut Power's phone rang. It was Watermelon Man. "Peanut Power, are you alright?

I ran Dalzell's name into the computer. Two years ago, his parents were shot by hunters. Dalzell hasn't been the same since!" said Watermelon Man.

"I must find and help him before he hurts someone else, or before someone hurts him," cried Peanut Power. He had only nine dogs left. Not many dogs when you have over 800 miles to go. "We need a lead dog! Which one of you would like to volunteer?" asked Peanut Power.

"I will be your new lead dog," barked Goober, wagging his tail like a big flag. "I know I can do it! Please give me a chance!"

Suddenly, sensing trouble, Goober ran to the top of a nearby gorge.

A thousand feet below, he saw Dalzell. Dalzell looked badly injured. "Are you okay?" yelled Goober into the abyss.

Dalzell shrieked, "My legs are broken! I can't move. I think the ledge I'm on is going to give way. Please help!"

Peanut Power had to think and act fast. He could not let Dalzell fall to his death. He summoned Supernut Power and Buckey Beaver. Buckey Beaver quickly gnawed down some trees and lashed together a sled big enough for Dalzell. Peanut Power then tied rope on the sled and connected the other end to Supernut Power's iron peanut. "Okay, Supernut Power, lower the sled down slowly," said Peanut Power.

While the sled was being lowered down the cliff, Propeller Man pressed against the ledge so it wouldn't give way. "I don't know how much longer I can hold up," cried Propeller Man.

"I think the ledge is going to give any minute now." Just as Peanut Power finished loading Dalzell into the sled, the ledge gave way. Peanut Power and Dalzell were hanging 2,000 feet above the ground. Supernut Power was giving it all his snowmobile had, but Peanut Power and Dalzell were too heavy for Supernut Power's iron peanut. "Hang on!" yelled Propeller Man, "We are going to fly first class to the top of the mountain." When Peanut Power and Dalzell reached the top of the mountain they both sighed with relief. Teamwork had saved them both.

"I am so sorry for being mean," wept Dalzell. "I just don't trust people. My parents were killed by hunters."

"I understand, Dalzell," replied Peanut Power. "I am sorry about your parents. But you are among friends now. Let us help you!"

Dalzell felt bad about attacking and delaying Peanut Power's team. "I am very sorry Peanut Power. I wish there was something I could do to make up the time you lost in the race."

"It's okay Dalzell," replied Peanut Power. "The dogs will heal. We haven't lost this race. We have gained a new friend."

At the Rohn Roadhouse checkpoint, Peanut Power sat down with his dogs and discussed a game plan to reach Nome quickly. Dalzell would be joining them.

Peanut Power made a sail for his sled to help with the added weight.

He was ready for the trail to Nome.

With slight hesitation, Peanut Power announced, "Goober will be our lead dog. He has the spunk and determination to do it. Will you take us to Nome, Goober?"

"Yes, Peanut Power!" cheered Goober, "I can do it!"

39

The team raced through Rohn dodging wild animals to Nikolai. There the villagers greeted them, and fed the whole team hot peanut soup. Afterward, they charged another 48 miles down the icy trail to McGrath. Peanut Power took his required 24-hour layover in McGrath. The dogs and Dalzell needed rest. While his dogs rested, Honeynut joined Peanut Power for a cozy candlelight dinner.

Dr. Bandage recommended changing the dogs' booties. Many of the dogs' feet were cut from the rugged terrain and sharp ice. While Dr. Bandage changed the dogs' booties, Dr. Quadruped inspected all the dogs with his stethoscope to make sure they were in good shape.

The team reached Takotna after another 23 miles. The villagers of Takotna had never seen such a small sled dog lead a team and pulling such a big moose. Next, they reached the ghost town of Ophir. The trail divided into a northern and southern route. "How do we know which trail to take?" questioned Goober.

"You always take the northern trail during the even-numbered years, and the southern trail during the odd-numbered years. So Goober, which trail will we be taking?" asked Peanut Power.

"We will be taking the southern route," said Goober, who was a dog who could count.

43

After a good meal of peanut stew, peanut butter muffins, and a short nap, the team once again started towards Nome. There were only 687 miles to go.

With the winds blowing, it took a matter of hours to reach Iditarod.

Iditarod looked spooky. "It looks like a ghost town," whispered Hazelnut. "It is a ghost town." said Peanut Power. "It was once a very busy town, full of miners looking to get rich. And a lot of them did. Now there's just abandoned buildings and rusted machinery left standing." Peanut Power wasn't the first musher to Iditarod. He had heard the first musher to win the halfway

prize would be jinxed and would have bad luck for the rest of the race.

Not wanting to rest in a ghost town, Peanut Power and his team pushed on. They pushed hard for 55 miles going up hills and down into creeks and valleys until they reached Shageluk. In Shageluk, Peanut Power took his first 8-hour mandatory stop. He changed his dogs' different colored booties and fed his team hot peanut broth. Peanut Power also tended to Dalzell who had slept most of the time. Dalzell did not look well. He needed to be flown to Nome. Without hesitation, Peanut Power called for help.

"Dr. Bandage, I need you to take another look at Dalzell. He doesn't look well," said Peanut Power.

"You're right! He needs medical attention. He needs to be flown to Nome. Bumping over the rough terrain is hard on his broken legs," said Dr. Bandage. And with that,

Propeller Man transported Dalzell to Nome.

"Good-bye, Dalzell! We're going to miss you!" shouted Peanut Power and his team.

At Anvik, the weather changed. The cold wind off the Yukon River sent shivers through Peanut

Power's body. It was so cold that frost started to grow on him and his dogs.

Peanut Power knew that his dogs loved the cold temperatures. Chestnut and Piñon teased him. "When we get cold, we like to roast by the campfire. If you get cold, Peanut Power, please tell us, we will keep you warm." Peanut Power didn't like the thought of roasting, or even getting burnt. He pushed on for another 18 miles until he reached Grayling.

While in Grayling, Peanut Power checked his GPS. The next 122 miles would be a challenge. The trail curved in and out like a snake from Grayling to Eagle Island and then to Kaltag. The route followed the twists and turns of the mighty Yukon.

Once in Kaltag, the dogs were dead tired. Little Goober, once a feisty pup, was now eager to bed down. He was no longer inter- ested in naps. He wanted to sleep. Peanut Power was tired, too. After feeding his dogs, he lay down next to his dogs and fell fast asleep.

The next morning, Peanut Power harnessed his dogs and pushed his team through high winds and piled snowdrifts over the Kaltag Portage for 85 miles until they reached Unalakleet, an Inupiaq village, located on the Bering Sea.

Seeing children, Goober became feisty again. "I love children!" said Goober, licking every face and hand he could reach.

"They love you too!" said Peanut Power. "You are a hero to them."

Peanut Power called Watermelon Man for an update. "What place are we in, Watermelon Man?" questioned Peanut Power.

"You are in 20th position and closing in fast. Did you know *The Nome Nugget* calls you a hero? They think you are the greatest for helping the mushers escape Dalzell. The veterinarians and PETA, an animal rights organization, appreciate you for helping Dalzell. You saved his life! Is there anything you want to tell the reporters?"

"You can tell *The Nome Nugget* we are doing fine. I am down to nine dogs. Nine determined dogs. I also have a fine lead dog," added Peanut Power, "His name is Goober."

After 40 more miles on the trail, the team reached Shaktoolik. There the team was treated to some peanut butter cookies baked by a junior high class. The cookies provided the quick energy the team needed to speed off to Koyuk. Peanut Power and his team were now in sixth place. Ahead of them were four-and five-time champions, not to mention some of the newer world sled dog racing champions.

There was another 48 miles from the icy terrain of Koyuk to Elim. Without wasting another breath, the dogs sped toward the village of Golovin. Within hours the team had traveled another 28 miles. Only 95 miles to go.

Peanut Power was getting tired. The dogs were out of wind too. Peanut Power wanted to rest, but sensed trouble from the north.

Sure enough, within minutes, a terrible blizzard struck. Many of the mushers decided to go on to Safety. They were willing to take a chance. They thought it was the strategy they needed to win the race.

Peanut Power stayed back thinking of his dogs and their safety.

The blizzard did not stop. It grew stronger by the hour. Propeller Man, Supernut Power, Buckey Beaver and all the race officials got off the trail and took cover. The windchill dropped to 90 degrees below zero. Snowdrifts covered the trail and trail markers.

The mushers needed help! Peanut Power called his sister, Peanut Puff. "Peanut Puff, I need your help!" pleaded Peanut Power. "Many of the mushers are in trouble."

"I will help you. I'm less than a minute away. I will blow the blizzard back to the North Pole," said Peanut Puff.

And with that, Peanut Puff, Peanut Power and his team headed into the storm. Peanut Puff blew as hard as she could and blew the blizzard away from the mushers. When the warm air hit the cold air it caused a whirlwind that carried the blizzard, Peanut Puff, Peanut Power and his team more than 100 miles down the trail. Peanut Puff had saved the mushers, but now Peanut Power and his team were 100 miles behind the leaders.

Peanut Power was disappointed that he had no chance of winning any of the prize money. However, he was happy that he had once again, with the help of his friends, aided those in need.

Little Goober was disappointed, too. "Goober, you have done well!" said Peanut Power. "You led the team as you said you would. We saved the mushers. You are the greatest!" Goober was happy to know he had really helped. He was now a hero.

Packing the sled, Peanut Power and his dogs headed for Nome. Within two hours they reached White Mountain where they gobbled a snack of peanut butter fudge and warmed themselves by the glow of a campfire. This was their last 8-hour mandatory stop. Fifty-five miles later they reached Safety. In Safety, they were greeted by their friends, Propeller Man and Watermelon Man. Propeller Man stated, "You are heroes! The mushers, spectators, and the people of Nome love you!" And with that, Watermelon Man shook Peanut Power's hand. "Although you will come in last, you have done it. You met the challenge and succeeded," exclaimed Watermelon Man.

A crowd of spectators waited for Peanut Power and his string of dogs. Off in the distance, Supernut Power saw Peanut Power. "It's them! It's Peanut Power and his dogs." Shouting and cheering, the crowd went wild as an exhausted Peanut Power and his team crossed under the burled arch.

There to greet them were Walnut, Filbert, Cashew, Almond, Dalzell and all of Peanut Power's friends.

All of the mushers gathered around Peanut Power and his dogs.

Peanut Power was standing next to his lead dog, Goober. Then one of the mushers approached Peanut Power. The people of Nome became quiet. The musher declared, "Peanut Power, the mushers and I want to thank you and your friends for saving our lives. We want to thank you for helping us get to Nome. You have done a wonderful deed."

Another musher added, "To show our appreciation for being a Good Samaritan, we would like to donate all our prize money to the sick children of Alaska."

The race committee gathered around Goober. The Mayor of Nome put a beautiful yellow flower lei around Goober's neck. He said, "Goober, you are the one responsible for getting your team to Nome. You are the winning lead dog, and because you are a champion — will you blow out the Widow's Lamp to show all the mushers are off the trail and the Iditarod is officially over for the year?" With a big smile, Goober blew out the Widow's Lamp. The crowd cheered as the flame was extinguished.

And with that, Peanut Power yelled to his dogs, "Almond, Brazil, Cashew, Chestnut, Filbert, Hazelnut, Hickory, Macadamia, Pecan, Piñon, Pistachio, Walnut and Goober—Time to board our flight back to Peanutville."

As Peanut Power started his takeoff, the people of Nome waved good-bye. Peanut Power waved good-bye too. Peanut Power and his team had done more than win "the last great race." Everyone had won.

PEANUT GLOSSARY

abyss – extremely deep or bottomless hole or crack in the Earth's surface

Anchorage – Alaska's largest city. Population is a little more than 291,000. The Ceremonial Start of the Iditarod takes place on the first Saturday of March every year in downtown Anchorage

antsy – restless or impatient

basket – body of sled used for carrying people or goods

blizzard – a violent snowstorm with high winds

booties – socks that protect a dog's feet from snow and ice balls

Burled Arch – marks the end of the Iditarod Trail Sled Dog Race, the finish line in Nome

ceremonial – a formal sequence of events to mark an important occasion

checkpoints – places along the trail where mushers have to check in. Mushers' first priority is to take care of their dogs

Dalzell Gorge – a dangerous steep stretch of trail between Rainy Pass and Rohn that leaves a lot of mushers and dog teams injured. A perfect name for a moose. Moose can threaten race teams

dog box – box on truck divided into sections used to transport dogs feisty – full of spirit; frisky

fraternal twins – one of a pair of twins who don't look like each other

gangline – a long rope to which each sled dog is attached by a neckline

gee – the command to turn right

gnawed – to bite or chew on

Good Samaritan – someone who goes out of their way to help others

GPS – a navigation system that uses satellites to pinpoint the exact location of a person. GPS is short for "global positioning system"

haw – the command to turn left

hike – the command for go

honorary musher – the Iditarod honors someone as a special way of thanking the person for contributing to the race or making a significant contribution to the dog racing sport. The person selected will wear Bib #1 and will ride in the Junior Iditarod Champion's sled down the ceremonial trail

husky – any northern-type dog

Iditarod – Iditarod was named from the Ingalik Indian word "Haiditarod," which means "a far distant place." Iditarod marks the official halfway point in the race

Iditarod Air Force – a team of local volunteer bush pilots who fly from checkpoint to checkpoint delivering straw bales, drop bags, food, checkpoint volunteers and dropped dogs

IditaRider – one who bids the highest amount of money to ride along in a musher's sled from the ceremonial start to the Campbell Airstrip

Iditarod Trail Sled Dog Race – organized in 1973 by mushing enthusiasts Joe Redington Sr. and Dorothy Page who were saddened by the declining use of dogsleds. They also wanted to preserve the historical Iditarod Trail between Seward and Nome

jinxed – to bring bad luck to

kibble – ground up meat or grain shaped into small dry pellets, dry pet food

lash – to bind or fasten with a rope, cord, etc.

lead dog – the dog at the front of the team that guides the team and takes orders from the driver. The lead dog must be smart and fast

litter – the offspring produced at birth, in this case puppies

mandatory stops – there are three mandatory rests each team must take during the Iditarod: one 24-hour layover to be taken at any checkpoint; one eight-hour layover, taken at any checkpoint on the Yukon River; and an eight-hour stop at White Mountain

microchip – tiny computer chip that is implanted under the skin of an animal for identification purposes

musher – driver of a team of sled dogs

mukluks – a soft warm boot lined with fur that is traditionally made of sealskin or reindeer skin

Nome – city at the end of the Iditarod Trail. Population is more than 3,800

Nome Nugget – a weekly newspaper published on Thursdays in Nome, Alaska. Alaska's oldest newspaper

PETA – an American organization that protects animals from suffering. PETA is the acronym for People for the Ethical Treatment of Animals

quadruped – an animal having four feet

red lantern – an award that goes to the last musher to cross the finish line. It is a symbol of perseverance and determination

runners – two long strips at the bottom of the sled that come in contact with the snow. The runners extend beyond the back of the sled for the mushers to stand on. Usually made of wood, covered with strips of plastic or Teflon

spectator – an observer of an event

stethoscope – a medical instrument for listening to the action of someone's heart, lungs, and breathing

strategy – a carefully developed plan of action for winning a race or achieving a goal

tundra – treeless plains of the Arctic region

veterinarian – a doctor that provides medical care to the dogs before, during, and after the race. A veterinarian is qualified to treat diseased or injured dogs and animals

village – a small community in a rural area, smaller than a town

whoa – command used to halt the team

widow's lamp – lamp lit at the restart of the race. When the last musher crosses the finish line it is extinguished. This symbolizes all mushers are off the trail and the Iditarod is completed for the year

Willow – a small community with a population just over 2,000. Willow is 70 miles north of Anchorage. Willow is the official host of the Iditarod Trail Sled Dog Race restart which is on the first Sunday in March

BASIC RACE RULES OF THE IDITAROD

RULE 1 - Musher Qualifications

A musher must be at least 18 years of age to race.

A musher must have completed a prior Iditarod Race; or completed the Yukon Quest International Sled Dog Race; or completed two 300-mile qualifiers and another approved qualifier for a total of 750 miles to be qualified to race in the Iditarod Trail Sled Dog Race.

RULE 2 - Race Start and Re-Start

The official starting date will be on the first Saturday in March, at 10 a.m. in Anchorage, Alaska. The re-start will be on the following Sunday in Willow. The race will begin at 2 p.m. Teams will leave the re-start line in the same order as they left in Anchorage.

RULE 3 - Checkpoints and Mandatory Stops

A musher must personally sign in at each checkpoint before continuing the race. This includes mandatory stops. A musher must take one mandatory stop at an official checkpoint. In addition, a musher must take one eight hour stop on the Yukon River, including Shageluk in odd numbered years, and one eight hour stop at White Mountain.

RULE 4 - Dog Maximums and Minimums

The maximum number of dogs a musher may start the race with is fourteen (14) dogs. A musher must have at least twelve (12) dogs on the line to start the race. At least five (5) dogs must be on the towline at the finish line.

RULE 5 - Mandatory Items

A musher must have with him/her the following items at all times: cold weather sleeping bag, ax, snowshoes, operational cooker, three gallon pot, fuel, veterinarian notebook, harness and cable gang-line, eight booties for each dog, and an insulated dog coat for each dog.

RULE 6 - Bib

A musher is required to wear his/her official Iditarod Trail Committee bib from the start and re-start. The bib may be carried from the White Mountain checkpoint to Safety checkpoint. The musher must wear the bib in a visible fashion from Safety checkpoint to Nome. The winner will continue to wear the bib through the lead dog ceremony.

RULE 7 - Good Samaritan Rule

A musher will not be penalized for being a Good Samaritan when aiding another musher in an emergency.

www.ingramcontent.com/pod-product-compliance
Lightning Source LLC
Chambersburg PA
CBHW041536240626
17164CB00002B/29